LOOK
AND
BE
GRATEFUL

TOMIE dePAOLA

HOLIDAY HOUSE
NEW YORK

OPEN
YOUR
EYES.

AND LOOK.

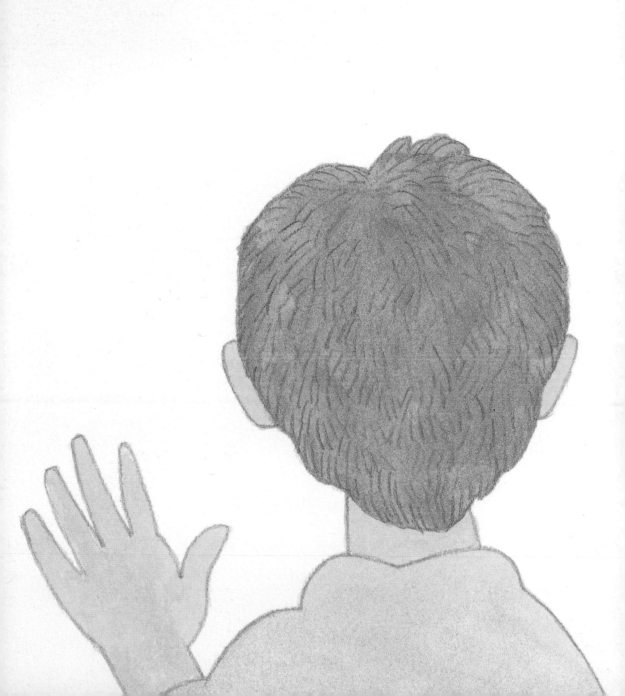

OPEN
YOUR
EYES,

AND
SEE,

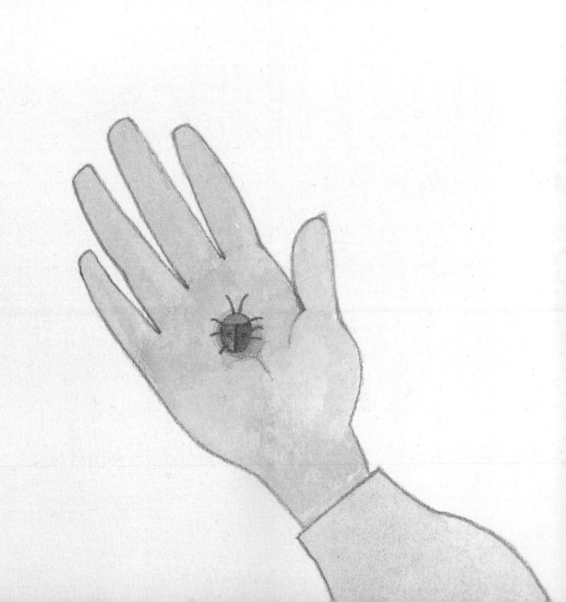

AND SAY

THANK

YOU,

FOR

TODAY

IS

TODAY.

BE GRATEFUL,

FOR
EVERYTHING
YOU
SEE.

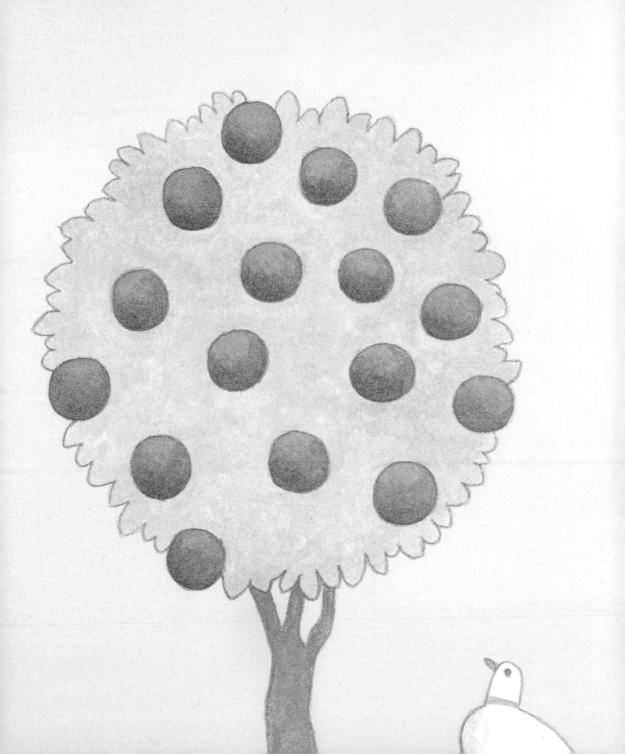

HAVE
GRATITUDE.

TODAY
IS
TODAY,

AND IT IS
A GIFT.

SO, BE GRATEFUL.

FOR ALL THE CHILDREN··
TdeP

Holiday House is registered in the U.S. Patent and Trademark Office.
Printed and Bound in April 2015 at Tien Wah Press, Johor Bahru, Johor, Malaysia.
The art for this book was created with transparent acrylics
on tea-stained Arches 150 pound paper.
www.holidayhouse.com
First Edition
1 3 5 7 9 10 8 6 4 2

Library of Congress Cataloging-in-Publication Data
DePaola, Tomie, 1934– author, illustrator.
Look and be grateful / by Tomie dePaola. — First edition.
pages cm
Summary: "A boy awakes with the dawn and
expresses gratitude for this unique day"— Provided by publisher.
ISBN 978-0-8234-3443-5 (hardcover)
[1. Gratitude—Fiction.] I. Title.
PZ7.D439Loo 2015
[E]—dc23
2014044525